4-3

MS GLEE WAS WAITING

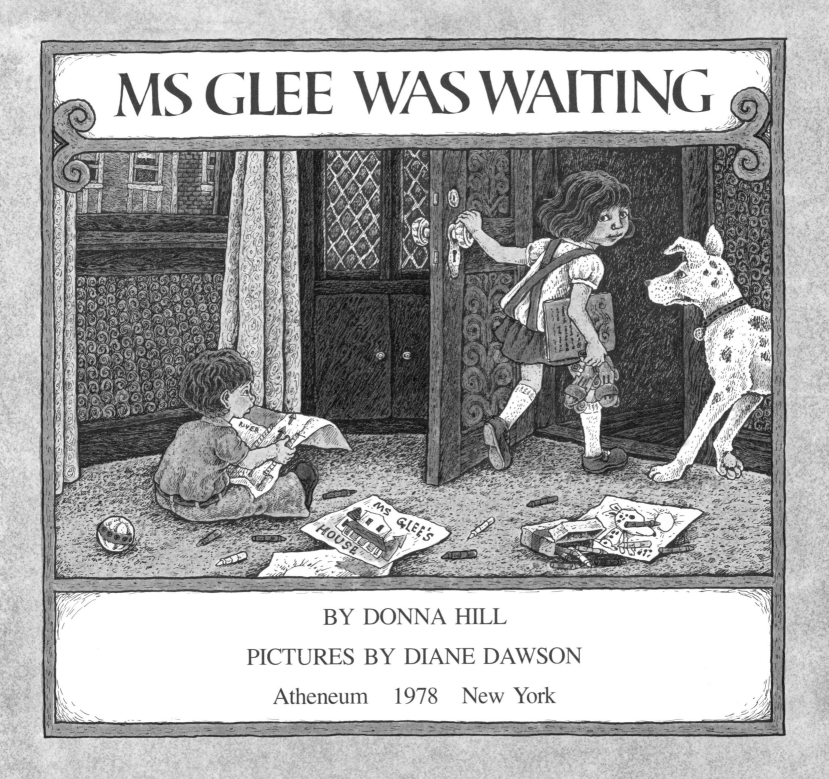

BY DONNA HILL

PICTURES BY DIANE DAWSON

Atheneum   1978   New York

Library of Congress Cataloging in Publication Data

Hill, Donna.   Ms. Glee was waiting.

SUMMARY: Laura finds many reasons why she
cannot attend her piano lesson.
I. Dawson, Diane.   II. Title.
PZ7.H549Ms   [E]   77-21137
ISBN 0-689-30618-0

Published simultaneously in Canada by McClelland & Stewart, Ltd.
Printed in the United States of America by
The Connecticut Printers, Hartford, Connecticut
Bound by A. Horowitz & Son / Bookbinders, Fairfield, New Jersey
First Edition

For Laura Lai who is Laura
And for David Lai who is her brother

Laura was late and Ms Glee was waiting,

so Laura put on her roller skates

but a skate strap broke,

so she brought out her wagon

but a wheel came loose,

so she borrowed a bike

but a tire went flat.

Laura whistled for a cab

but the cab ran out of gas,

so she got on a bus

but the bus broke down,

so she climbed on a train

but the train got derailed.

She boarded a tugboat

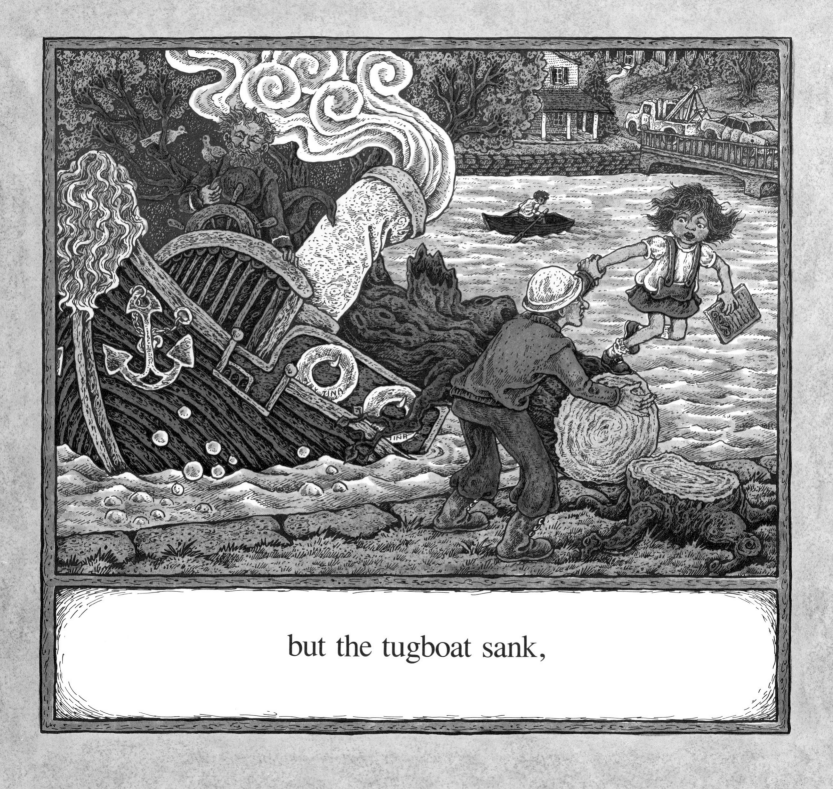

but the tugboat sank,

so she hired a balloon

but the air leaked out,

so she bargained for a litter

but the litter-bearers got into a fight.

She jumped into a gondola

but the oarsman fell off,

so she took a jinriksha

but the runner stubbed his toe,

so she called for a howdah

but the elephant stopped for a bite to eat.

Laura had to get there because
Ms Glee was waiting, so she ran.

But she got a blister and had to go back home
for a Band-Aid. By then of course it was too late.

That is why Laura never did get
to Ms Glee's piano lesson.

So she said.